Rackham's
FAIRY TALE
COLORING BOOK

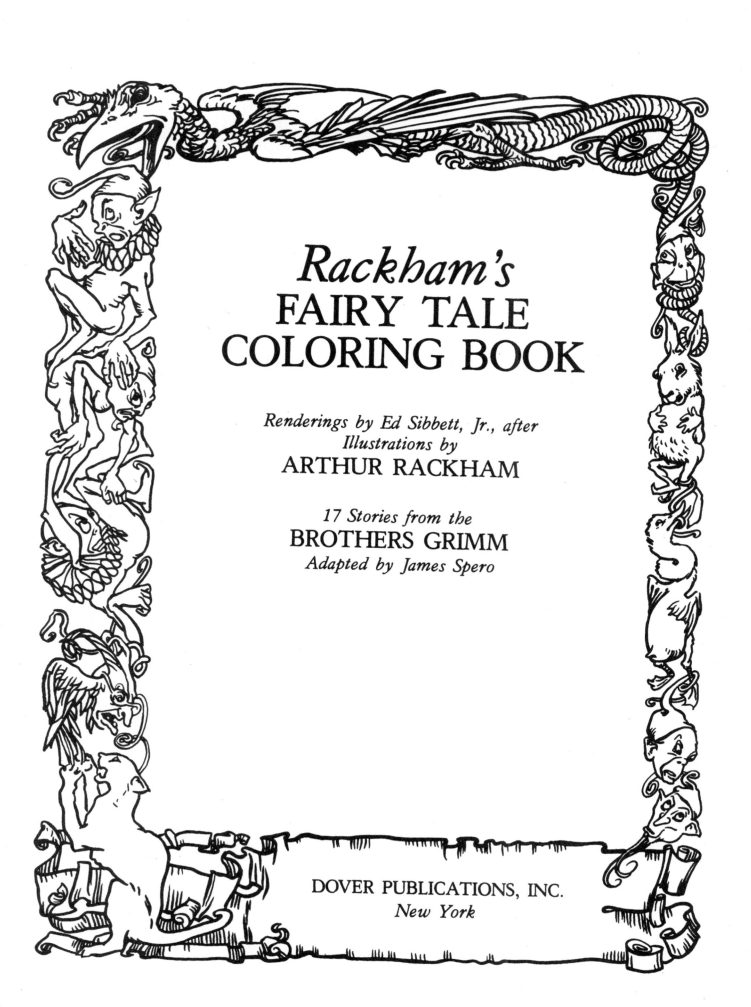

Rackham's FAIRY TALE COLORING BOOK

Renderings by Ed Sibbett, Jr., after
Illustrations by
ARTHUR RACKHAM

17 Stories from the
BROTHERS GRIMM
Adapted by James Spero

DOVER PUBLICATIONS, INC.
New York

Contents

HANSEL AND GRETEL   3

LITTLE RED RIDING-HOOD   10

RUMPELSTILTSKIN   14

THE LITTLE FARMER   18

SNOW WHITE   22

DOCTOR KNOW-ALL   28

THE GOOSE GIRL   30

THE FOUR CLEVER BROTHERS   34

THE FOX AND THE HORSE   39

KING THRUSHBEARD   42

SLEEPING BEAUTY   45

RAPUNZEL   50

CAT AND MOUSE IN PARTNERSHIP   53

FUNDEVOGEL   56

THE VALIANT LITTLE TAILOR   58

THE QUEEN BEE   60

THE LADY AND THE LION   62

For Elizabeth, with thanks.
E. S.

Bibliographical Note

Rackham's Fairy Tale Coloring Book is a new work, first published by Dover Publications, Inc., in 1979.

International Standard Book Number
ISBN-13: 978-0-486-23844-9
ISBN-10: 0-486-23844-X

Manufactured in the United States by Courier Corporation
23844X15
www.doverpublications.com

Hansel and Gretel

MANY YEARS AGO, on the edge of a great forest, there lived a poor woodcutter, his cruel wife and their two children, a little boy named Hansel and a little girl named Gretel. The family had almost no money at all, and times were hard. One night, when the wife could not sleep because of her hunger, she said to the woodcutter, ''Starvation stares us in the face. We have but little food left—there is not enough for the whole family. In order for us to survive, we must take the children deep into the forest tomorrow and leave them there. The wild beasts will make short work of them.'' The woodcutter did not want to do this, for he truly loved his children. ''Then you might was well start making coffins for the four of us,'' said the hardhearted woman, forcing him to agree.

By chance little Hansel was lying awake in bed nearby, and overheard all. He woke Gretel and told her what was in store for them. She began to cry, but Hansel told her to be brave and promised that he would take care of them. Quietly he slipped out of the house and gathered little white pebbles, hiding them in his pockets. Then he went back to bed.

The next morning, the woodcutter's wife awoke the children and told them that they were to come along on the day's work. She gave them some bread to take with them. As they went along, Hansel secretly marked the path by dropping the little white stones from his pockets. When they reached a spot deep in the forest that the children had never seen before, the woodcutter and his wife stopped. "Now, children," she said, "gather up some twigs so we can make a nice fire." This was done, and once the fire was blazing, she said, "Now your father and I will chop wood. While we are away, rest by the fire and eat your bread." Having eaten, the children's eyes became heavy, and soon they were asleep. The woodcutter and his wife slipped away, leaving the children alone.

When Hansel and Gretel awoke, it was the middle of the night. The air was filled with the growls and snarls of animals hidden by the darkness. Gretel grew afraid, but Hansel reassured her. The moon came out and the pebbles that Hansel had dropped shone like silver. By following them, the children were quickly led back to their house. They knocked at the door.

Their mother was surprised to see them again, and scolded them for having gotten lost, even though it was not their fault. The woodcutter was glad that they had returned, for his heart had been heavy without them. But their mother was just as set on being rid of them as ever. That night, when she thought the children were asleep, she again forced her husband to agree to lose them in the forest. As before, the children overheard her cruel plan.

The next day Hansel was given some bread for provision and the family went out into the forest. This time they went deeper than any of them had ever gone before. Hansel dropped bread crumbs to mark the path. A fire was lighted and the children were left to sleep. At night, when they awoke, they searched for the crumbs to guide them back. But they were gone! The hungry birds of the forest had eaten every one.

For two days Hansel and Gretel wandered about the forest, trying to find their way back. But they only became more and more lost. They

managed to live on the few berries they were able to pick. When they were about to give up hope they suddenly smelled something—something wonderful and delicious. Following their noses, they soon found themselves standing in front of a little house made entirely of candies and cakes! The roof was made of cakes and the windows were of transparent sugar. Hansel and Gretel could not help themselves. Gretel started to eat part of the roof and Hansel ate one of the windows.

As they ate, they heard a little voice inside the house say, ''Nibble, nibble, mousie! Who's nibbling at my housie?'' But the children thought it was only the wind they heard, and kept on eating.

All at once the door opened and an aged woman came out of the house. Very sweetly she asked Hansel and Gretel inside. There she fed them on pancakes and berries and cream, while they told her of their adventures. Then she tucked them into the softest little beds they had ever slept in, saying that they need not be afraid, for they could stay with her.

Poor children! They did not know that they had fallen into the hands of Rosina Sweettooth, a wicked witch who enticed unwary children with her mouth-watering house and then baked and ate them! The next morning Rosina woke up Hansel and, before he knew it, pushed him into the stable and locked him there, ignoring his cries. Then she shook Gretel awake. ''Get up, get up, you lazy thing!'' she cried. ''Go down to the kitchen and cook a dainty treat for your brother. We must fatten him, and when he is nice and plump, I'll eat him.'' She smacked her lips. Gretel went about her tasks, for the poor girl had no choice.

Now it is a well-known fact that witches have very bad eyesight. Every day Rosina went to the stable to see if Hansel was getting any fatter by

squeezing his finger to feel how thick it was. Hansel had found an old chicken bone, and gave it to Rosina to touch, and she did not realize that she was being tricked.

For weeks she waited, hoping that Hansel would become plump and succulent. But his finger always felt skinny! Then she lost patience. ''Gretel,'' she said one day, ''get the oven ready and fetch water for cooking, for tomorrow I shall dine on Hansel! First polish the silver and fold the napkins. Then heat the oven and knead the dough and we will do our baking.'' The helpless Gretel made the dough ready. ''Is the oven hot?'' the witch asked. ''I don't know,'' said Gretel. ''Silly girl,'' snapped Rosina, ''Open up the door and crawl into the oven a bit so we can find out.'' The evil Rosina actually wanted to get Gretel into the oven and then slam the door behind her so she could cook her and eat her before she ate Hansel!

But Gretel was crafty. ''How do you get into the oven?'' she asked. ''Like this,'' said the witch, who bent over and stuck her head inside the oven. At once Gretel gave her a shove so that she went right in and then slammed and locked the door behind her. And that was the end of Rosina Sweettooth.

Gretel ran to free Hansel from the stable and the two children went through the witch's house. To their amazement, they found gold, silver and precious jewels. Eagerly they crammed their pockets full of the treasure. Then they broke off pieces of the house to feed themselves as they tried to find their way back home.

In high hopes Hansel and Gretel set out into the forest. They wandered and wandered and after many days and many adventures, were able to find their way back to their house. When they knocked at the door, their father

greeted them with open arms, for he had been sick at heart from missing them. Their cruel mother had died and now, with the treasure they had gathered from the witch's house, the family was able to live together happily for the rest of their lives.

Little Red Riding-Hood

ONCE UPON A TIME there was a little girl who was greatly loved by all who knew her. Her grandmother, who lived in the forest, had given her a cloak of red velvet. The little girl wore it all the time, so that she became known as Little Red Riding-Hood.

It happened that one day her grandmother fell ill. Hearing of it, Little Red Riding-Hood's mother prepared a basket of food for her to take to the old woman. As the little girl went out the door, her mother warned her to go straight to her grandmother's without speaking to strangers or stopping along the way.

Little Red Riding-Hood was making her way through the forest when a wolf popped out of a thicket and greeted her. Little Red Riding-Hood was a friendly child, and not knowing that wolves are dangerous and not to be trusted, she ignored her mother's warnings and told him that she was bringing a basket of food to her grandmother, who was ill. The wolf said he hoped her grandmother would soon be feeling better, and then suggested that the child pick some flowers, which would surely cheer the old woman up even more. Little Red Riding-Hood thought that was a fine idea, and started to gather wild flowers.

While she was doing this, the wolf ran ahead and knocked on the grandmother's door. "Who is there?" called the old woman from her bed. The wolf disguised his voice and replied, "It is Little Red Riding-Hood, with a

basket of food my mother has sent you." "Open the latch and come in, my dear," said the grandmother. With this the wolf opened the door, ran into the house, leapt into the bed and swallowed the grandmother whole, in a single gulp. Then the sly animal put on the grandmother's glasses, cap and shawl and waited in the bed.

Soon there came a knock at the door. Again the wolf disguised his voice, this time making it seem like the grandmother's. "Who is it," he called out. "It is Little Red Riding-Hood, grandmother," she replied. "Come in, my sweet. The door is open," said the wolf. Little Red Riding-Hood slowly came in. "And what have you brought me, my pet?" asked the wolf. "A basket of food from my mother and some flowers I picked in the woods," she replied. "Come near the bed, my dear, and let me see them," said the wolf, whose mouth was already beginning to water at the thought of eating the little girl. Little Red Riding-Hood drew near the bed. "Grandmother, what big ears you have," she said. "All the better to hear you with, my dear," replied the wolf. "And grandmother, what big eyes you have," she said. "All the better to see you with," replied the wolf. "And grandmother, what big teeth you have," she said. "All the better to eat you with!" cried the wolf as he jumped out of bed and ate the child with a single gulp.

Just then a woodsman happened to be passing. He heard the noise in the grandmother's house and went to see what was happening. When he saw the wolf, he chased after it, swinging his sharp ax. With one blow he cut the evil animal in two and out jumped Little Red Riding-Hood and her grandmother, both unharmed. They thanked the woodsman and all three sat down to enjoy the food Little Red Riding-Hood's mother had sent. Never again did Little Red Riding-Hood ignore her mother's warnings.

Rumpelstiltskin

THERE ONCE LIVED a poor miller who was blessed with a beautiful daughter. One day he saw the king passing by. Thinking that he might be able to better his daughter's lot in life, the miller ran to the king. ''Sire,'' he said, ''I have a daughter who can spin straw into the finest gold.'' The king's eyes opened wide. ''This interests me greatly. Tonight come to the castle with your daughter.''

When the two appeared at the castle, the king led the miller's daughter to a room in which there was a spinning wheel and a pile of straw. ''Your father tells me you can spin gold from straw,'' he said. ''Spin through the night. If the straw in this room has not all been spun into gold by morning, you will die.'' He went out, locking the door behind him.

The poor girl began to weep and wring her hands, for she had no idea of how to spin straw into gold. Suddenly the door flew open and a very strange-looking little man walked into the room.

''Good evening, mistress,'' he said. ''Why are you weeping so?'' ''Alas,'' she sobbed, ''either I spin this straw into gold tonight, or I lose my life.'' ''If I were to spin the straw into gold for you, what would you give me?'' he asked. ''The necklace I am wearing,'' replied the miller's daughter. The little man took the necklace and sat down at the spinning wheel. Whirrr! Whirrr! He spun until all the straw had been spun into gold. Then he left, as mysteriously as he had come.

The next morning the king was astounded to find the room full of glistening gold. But that only made things worse for the miller's daughter, for that night the king took her to a larger room with even more straw and left her alone with the same threats. The door opened and in strolled the mysterious little man. ''And *now* what are you weeping over?'' he asked. ''Alas,'' she said, ''once again the straw must be spun into gold,'' ''I will spin it for you if you give me the ring on your finger,'' said the little man, and to this the miller's daughter agreed. So he sat down at the spinning wheel and—whirrr! whirrr!—the straw was all spun into gold by morning.

How pleased the king was to find all the gold! And how distressed the miller's daughter was when the king took her that night to an even larger room filled with even more straw! This time he said to her, ''Spin all the straw by morning and, as a reward, I shall make you my queen. But should you fail, you lose your life.'' The miller's daughter sat in utter despair. When the little man appeared, she told him how her problems had grown. ''And now,'' she sobbed, ''I must have the straw spun into gold, but I have nothing left to offer you.'' ''If I spin the straw into gold for you, you will become queen,'' replied the little man. ''If you become queen, you will have a child. If you promise that you will give that baby to me, I will spin for you tonight.'' The miller's daughter had no choice and made the promise.

In the morning the king was amazed to find all the piles of gold. He kept his word to the miller's daughter and made her his queen. For a year

the two lived happily. Then the queen had a child. She had quite forgotten the strange little man, so she was shocked when one day he suddenly appeared before her, demanding the child that had been promised to him. The queen wept and wailed, and begged him to accept anything else in the kingdom instead of the child. The little man was moved by her tears, and finally said, ''I will let you keep your child if you can discover my name.'' When he left, the queen ordered that a list be made of every name of every subject in the kingdom. This was done, and when the little man returned, she read off the names it contained.

''Is your name Frank?'' she asked. ''No,'' he answered. ''Is it Alfred?'' ''No.'' ''Peter or James?'' ''No. No.'' ''Cyril, Gordon, Jacob, Julius, Alexander or Oscar?'' ''None of those.'' On and on the poor queen went, until she reached the bottom of the list. The little man's name remained a secret. He left, promising to come back for one last chance.

The queen sent out messengers to try to learn the little man's name, and it was only through a lucky chance that one returned to her and said, ''Your majesty, as I was passing through the woods I saw a most fantastic little man dancing around a fire and singing this song to himself:

'Today I'll bake and tomorrow brew beer,

So all will be ready when I bring the babe here.

For the Queen doesn't know, to her sorrow and shame,

That RUMPELSTILTSKIN is my name!' ''

When the little man came to see the queen for the last time, she looked him straight in the eye and said, ''Is your name Tom?'' ''No.'' ''Then is it Dick?'' ''No.'' ''Harry?'' ''No.'' ''Then perhaps it is Rumpelstiltskin.'' The little man shrieked in rage and jumped up and down on the floor so hard that he fell through and was never heard of again.

The Little Farmer

A LITTLE FARMER once lived with his wife in great poverty. They were laughed at by their heartless neighbors, who were far more fortunate than they. One day their hunger became so great that the farmer and his wife slaughtered their only cow and salted the meat.

The little farmer decided to take the cow's hide to the market in town to see if he could get a good price for it. On the way, he found a raven who had broken its wing. The farmer was a kind man and took pity on the wretched creature, set the wing, wrapped the bird in the hide and took it along with him. It was almost night when a fierce storm arose. The little farmer ran to a mill for shelter. He pounded on the door, which was opened by the miller's wife. The law of hospitality to the helpless traveler is strong, and she let the little farmer in, explaining that her husband had gone away on business.

The miller's wife showed the little farmer to a bed of straw. He lay down, with the hide next to him. When the miller's wife thought he was in a sleep so deep that nothing would wake him up, she opened the door and in walked a man in black. ''My husband is not at home,'' she said to him. ''Let us sit down and have a feast.'' She spread the table with meats and opened a bottle of wine and the two began to eat and laugh. But the little farmer was awake, and heard and saw all.

Suddenly the miller's wife heard footsteps approaching. "It is my husband," she cried. "Quick, hide!" The man in black ran into the linen chest and closed the lid on top of him. The miller's wife hid the meat under the pillow and the wine under the bed. Then she ran to the door and opened it for her husband. Weary and dripping rain, the miller came in. "Good evening, my dearest," she said. "How was your day?" "Hard," he answered. "And I am very hungry indeed. I hope you have something good to eat." "Only cheese and water," lied his wife.

The miller noticed the little farmer, and his wife told him how he came to be there. The miller woke him and invited him to share their bread and cheese. Then the miller noticed the hide with the raven in it. "What is that bird?" he asked. "Ah," said the little farmer, "that raven is a prophet, and can tell me three things." "Can you show us how he does this?" asked the miller. "Of course," said the farmer, and he pinched the raven so that it cawed. "It tells me there is wine under the bed," said the little farmer. The miller looked, and there it was. The little farmer pinched the raven again. "It says there is meat under the pillow," said the little farmer. The miller looked, and there it was. When he pinched the raven a third time, the farmer frowned. "The third thing is terrible. You had best not know of it," he said. But the miller insisted, promising the little farmer three hundred gold coins if he would tell.

The farmer consented, and told the miller and his wife, "The raven says there is a devil in the linen chest." And with that, the man in black bounded out of the linen chest and tore out of the door as fast as his legs would carry him. The amazed miller gave the little farmer his three hundred gold coins, and he went home a rich man.

When the little farmer's neighbors asked him how he came by so much money, he told them he had got it from selling his cow's hide. So his greedy neighbors, thinking they would make themselves richer, skinned all their cows. But when they took the hides to market, they found they were worth almost nothing!

The neighbors were so furious when they came back that they decided to punish the little farmer for his lie. They captured him and told him that they were going to seal him in a barrel and roll it into the lake nearby. They went away to get ready, and the little farmer was left to ponder his fate. Just then a shepherd passed by with his flock. "What are you doing?" the shepherd asked. "Oh, my neighbors wanted to make me bailiff," the little farmer explained. "But to get the post, a person must first climb into that barrel, which I don't want to do." The shepherd told him that he was a fool to turn down so great a post and, deserting his flock, got in himself. Quickly the little farmer nailed the top on and then hid himself. When the evil neighbors came back, they rolled the barrel right into the lake.

How surprised they were when the little farmer soon walked by, driving the shepherd's flock before him. "Why, little farmer," they all asked, "how did you manage to return with this flock?" "When the barrel hit the bottom of the lake," he explained, "I forced open the top and found myself in a beautiful land of rolling hills, filled with sheep." "Are there any remaining there?" they asked. "Why, yes," he replied. "Just waiting to be taken up to land."

The greedy neighbors rushed to the lake. Looking on its smooth, mirror-like surface, they saw the fleecy clouds in the sky reflected in the water. The fools thought that they were looking at sheep in the lake and went plunging in headlong. They were all drowned, and the little farmer and his wife lived the rest of their lives in peace and contentment.

Snow White

ON A SNOWY EVENING, many years ago, a queen sat at a window, sewing. She pricked her finger with her needle, and three drops of blood fell upon the black windowsill. The queen sighed. "If only I could have a child whose skin was white as the snow, whose cheeks were red as my blood, whose hair was black as the windowsill," she said.

Not long after, the queen did have such a child, and she was named Snow White. Then the queen died. Snow White's father soon married again, to a woman who was as cruel as she was beautiful. One of her possessions was a magic mirror. Every night she sat before it and asked it this question, "Mirror, mirror, on the wall, who is fairest of them all?" And the mirror always replied, "You are, my queen."

But Snow White grew lovelier every day, until she was more beautiful than the queen. So it happened that one night, when the queen went before the mirror, it told her, "My queen, that thou art passing fair, 'tis true. But Snow White fairer is than you." Rage and jealousy ate at the evil woman's heart.

The queen instructed one of the royal huntsmen to take Snow White deep into the forest, slay her and bring back her heart as a sign that she was really dead. Sadly the huntsman set about his terrible task. When he and Snow White had walked for miles into the forest, the huntsman drew his knife and told the terrified girl to prepare to die. Snow White begged him to spare her life, promising that she would take refuge in the forest and never be seen by him or the queen again. Moved by her great beauty, the huntsman agreed, and Snow White fled. Then the huntsman killed a passing deer, cut out its heart and took it back to the queen, saying it was Snow White's. The queen was content.

Snow White, meanwhile, was running through the forest. The poor child ran until evening, when she found a little house and entered it, exhausted. There she found a table set with seven places, and seven little beds. She threw herself onto one and fell asleep.

Soon the door opened, and in came seven dwarfs. The house was theirs, and they earned a living by mining copper and gold. Seeing Snow White, they were charmed by her great beauty. When she awoke, she found herself surrounded by the seven men. She told them of the adventure that had led her to their house. "Will you cook for us?" asked one. "And clean for us?" asked another. "And sew for us?" asked another. "Yes, I will," said Snow White, and the seven dwarfs agreed to let her live with them. "But take care," they warned her. "Some day the queen is bound to find out that you are still alive, and will try to kill you. When we are at work in the mine, stay inside and open the door to no one."

One day the queen stood before her mirror and asked the question, "Mirror, mirror, on the wall, who is fairest of them all?" And the mirror replied, "Queen, that thou art passing fair 'tis true, but Snow White, living in the forest glen, with the seven little men, is a thousand times more fair than you." The furious queen at once set about her revenge. With great craft she disguised herself as an old peddler woman and made her way into the forest. When she drew near the cottage of the seven dwarfs, she called out, "Fine belts for sale. Buy my belts of the finest leather."

The temptation was too much for Snow White, and she invited the old hag inside to show her belts. When she tried one on, the wicked queen pulled it so tight that Snow White lost her breath and fell down as though dead. Thinking that she had rid herself of Snow White, the queen went back to the castle. The dwarfs were frantic when they found Snow White. Quickly they loosened the belt, and Snow White was able to breathe again. They made her promise never to open the door to anyone.

Meanwhile, the queen had gone in front of her mirror and found that her scheme had failed. The next day she disguised herself as another peddler woman and used her magic arts to poison a comb. When she returned to the house of the seven dwarfs, she began to cry her wares. Snow White could not resist. She opened a window and looked out. "Buy my goods," croaked the evil queen. "For example, this lovely comb." She held up the comb. Snow White sighed, "Alas, I am forbidden to let anyone in." The queen smiled a toothless smile. "Why, my dear," she said, "you don't even have to let me into the house. I will hand it to you through the window." Snow White took the comb and the second she put it to her hair, she fell as though dead. The queen laughed and went back to the castle.

When the dwarfs returned home and found Snow White on the floor, they rushed to her. Lifting her, they knocked the comb out of her hair and she regained her senses. The dwarfs cautioned her even more severely to be on her guard.

The queen soon found out that her plan had again failed, so she devised a cunning disguise that made her look like an old farmer's wife. Then she used all her magic to make a poisoned apple. One side of it was a tempting

red, the other green. She put it in a basket with other apples and made her way to the dwarfs' house and knocked on the door. "Buy my apples, my pretty?" she called to Snow White. "I cannot," she replied. "Never mind," said the queen. "I will give you an apple free." She held out the poisoned apple. "It looks so delicious," Snow White said, "but I dare not eat, for it might be poisoned." "Nonsense," cried the queen, and she took a bite of the green side herself. The crafty woman had poisoned the red side only. Thinking that she had nothing to fear, Snow White took a bite out of the red side. Immediately she fell as though dead. The queen went back to the castle, content that her plan had finally worked.

Try as they would, this time the dwarfs were unable to revive Snow White, and sorrowfully they gave her up as dead. But they could not bear the thought of never seeing her again, so they put her in a glass coffin, which they placed in the middle of the forest.

One day a prince came upon the glass coffin as he was riding through the forest. When he saw Snow White, who looked as though she were only asleep, he thought she was the most beautiful person he had ever seen. He begged the dwarfs to give him the glass coffin, telling them that if he did not have it, he would surely die. The kind dwarfs could not refuse his request, although the thought of parting with Snow White caused them great grief. As they lifted the coffin, they stumbled and the piece of the apple that had been caught in Snow White's throat popped out. To their amazement, she revived.

The prince was overjoyed and asked Snow White if she would become his bride. She willingly consented. As for the queen—at the wedding banquet, she was forced to dance in red-hot iron shoes until she fell dead.

Doctor Know-All

A POOR FARMER named Crabb was once taking a load of wood in a cart drawn by two oxen. He sold it to a doctor and, seeing how prosperous the man was, asked him if it was difficult to join his profession. ''Not at all,'' said the doctor. ''Just sell your oxen and buy a fine suit of clothes and have a sign made that says 'Dr. Know-All' and hang it outside your door. Also buy an ABC book with a picture of a rooster in it.'' Crabb followed his advice and his practice prospered.

One day there came to Crabb a duke whose money had been stolen. He asked the doctor to come to his castle and help him find the thieves. The doctor consented and went with his wife. When they arrived, they sat down to dinner. A servant came in with a dish, and Crabb said to his wife, ''Here is the first,'' meaning the first course. The servant, however, thought that the doctor was pointing him out as the first thief, which he indeed was.

When a second servant approached bearing a covered platter, the doctor said, ''Here is the second,'' and the servant thought *his* secret was known, for he was guilty as well. Then the duke asked the doctor if he could tell him what was in the covered platter. ''O, wretched Crabb!'' moaned the doctor, certain his ignorance would be discovered. The duke was amazed, for crabs were indeed the dish being served!

Then the doctor took out his ABC book. ''And now I will tell you where your stolen money is hidden,'' he said as he began to thumb through

the pages. But he was unable to find the picture of the rooster and, losing his temper, cried, ''Come out, come out, I know you're in there!'' Now it happened that a third servant was hiding in a closet and, thinking the game was up, came out with the money and confessed all, as did the other two servants.

The fame of Dr. Know-All soon spread throughout the country, and little Crabb, who had been so poor, lived in comfort for the rest of his life.

The Goose Girl

MANY YEARS AGO there lived a queen whose king had died some years before. She had one daughter, whom she loved very much. When the princess reached the age when she should wed, a marriage was arranged with a prince in a neighboring kingdom. The queen sorrowfully sent her daughter off on the horse Falada, who could speak, and had her accompanied by a lady-in-waiting.

After the two were well on their way, the lady-in-waiting forced the princess to dismount. She made her exchange her clothing, and mounted Falada herself, threatening to kill the princess if she ever revealed that they had changed places. When the two arrived at their destination, the lady-in-waiting was received by the king as though she were the princess, and a day was set for the wedding. The lady-in-waiting told the king that the princess was an idle girl she had met along the way. The king decided he would find work for her, and had her help Conrad, the boy who tended the royal gaggle of geese.

But the lady-in-waiting feared that Falada would reveal the truth, and had the animal beheaded. The woeful princess was able to buy the head, and hung it in the dark gateway through which she had to pass every day as she took the geese into the fields. Looking at it, she said, ''Alas, Falada, there you hang.'' The head replied, ''Alas, my princess, it gives me a pang to see you in a state so low. I pray your mother may never know.''

When the princess and Conrad reached the fields with the geese, the princess sat down and untied her beautiful golden hair. It spilled over her shoulders, and Conrad tried to take some of it. But she whispered to the breezes, "Wind, toss Conrad's hat in air. Make him run after it, as I comb my tresses and sit, till I have done up all my hair." And as she asked, so it happened.

Now for three days the same events passed. Three times she spoke with the head of Falada, three times she had the wind carry off Conrad's hat. When Conrad told the king of this, the king decided he had to see for himself, and followed her the next day. Things went just as before.

The king was puzzled and called the princess before him. "Who are you, and why do you act so?" he asked her. "I may not tell you, for I fear for my life," she replied. "Then tell the oven," said the king. He took her to the great oven, which was empty and cold, and let her get in. Thinking herself alone, the princess began to weep. "Alas," she sobbed, "look at me, a princess, alone and forgotten in the world. A wicked lady-in-waiting forced me to change places with her. Now I am no better than a goose girl. That things should come to such a pass!" But the king was standing nearby, and heard everything the princess said. When she came out of the oven, he kissed her on the forehead and had her taken to a room where she was dressed in a rich gown and jewels.

That night the king gave a banquet. Both the lady-in-waiting and the princess were there, but the lady-in-waiting did not recognize the princess because of the finery she was wearing. At the end of the meal, the king asked the lady-in-waiting, "What would you do with a person who deceives his master, lies and causes suffering?" "Why, I should have him put into a barrel studded with nails, and have the barrel dragged through the streets by

two white horses until he is dead,'' she replied. ''You have pronounced your own sentence,'' said the king, and the lady-in-waiting was put to death. Afterwards the prince and princess were wed, and they lived in peace and great happiness for the rest of their lives.

The Four Clever Brothers

IN A FARAWAY KINGDOM there once dwelt a poor man with four sons. When they came of age, the father gathered them together and spoke to them thus, ''My dearest children, I have nothing more to give you—you must go forth into the world and learn useful trades. But this day four years from now, come back to me so that I may see how you have fared.'' So the four brothers walked along the road, and when they came to the crossroads, each one went in a different direction, waving goodbye to the others.

At the end of the four years, the brothers returned home and joyously embraced each other. Their father asked them what trades they had learned. The first had become a stargazer, the second a clever thief, the third a huntsman and the fourth a tailor. The father decided to put them to the test.

Taking them into the forest, the father stopped some distance from a tall tree. He turned to the stargazer and said, ''Tell me what is in the tree.'' The stargazer took his telescope, through which he could see anything happening in the sky or on earth, and looked into it. ''I see a finch's nest with five eggs in it,'' he said. Then the father turned to the thief. ''Climb the tree and steal the eggs without disturbing the mother finch,'' he said. The thief did it without any problem, for he could take whatever he pleased without anyone knowing of it.

Turning to the huntsman, the father ordered him to shoot through the

five eggs with one shot. He took aim with the gun, which never missed its target, and fired one bullet through the five eggs. Now the father turned to the tailor. ''Sew the eggs together,'' he ordered. The tailor had a needle that would sew anything together, and deftly he sewed the shells of the eggs back together again. So well did he do the job that three days later the eggs hatched, and the little birds were fine, save for a thin red line about their throats.

The father was pleased with his sons and said, ''My boys, you have all done well. I hardly know who is the cleverest of you. I can only hope that you will be able to prove yourselves in the world.''

Not long afterwards it happened that a monstrous dragon carried off the only daughter of the king. The grief-stricken monarch made a decree that was posted and read throughout the kingdom. Any hero who rescued the princess would be given her hand in marriage. The four brothers saw their chance and took it.

Looking through his telescope, the stargazer was able to find the princess. The dragon had taken her to a rock in the middle of the sea, and there kept her prisoner. The brothers went to the king and told him where his daughter was. The king gave them a boat and begged them to try their best to save his child.

The four brothers rowed and rowed until they were near the dragon's rock. As they approached, the huntsman picked up his gun and took aim. Then he lowered his gun. ''I cannot shoot,'' he said, ''for the dragon is lying with his head in the lap of the princess. If I shoot him, I fear she will be shot as well.'' ''That's no problem at all,'' said the thief, who deftly managed to steal the princess from under the sleeping dragon.

The four brothers and the princess were rowing away when the dragon awoke with a start. Furious, he went flying through the air to regain his lost treasure. The huntsman took aim and shot the beast right through the heart. The monster fell into the sea, and so huge was its body that, when it hit the water, the wave it made smashed the boat to little pieces. Desperately the four brothers and the princess swam in the wreckage. The tailor pulled out his needle and quickly stitched the pieces of the boat together again. They were then able to return to land safely.

The king showered his daughter with kisses, and told the four brothers that he would keep his word. ''But which of you,'' he asked, ''will wed my daughter?'' ''She will wed me,'' said the stargazer, ''for had I not seen her with my telescope, she would still be on that wretched island with the dragon.'' ''No, she will wed *me*,'' said the thief, ''for had I not taken her from the dragon, she would be sitting there this very minute.'' ''You are *all* wrong,'' exclaimed the huntsman. ''It was I who saved her from the dragon by slaying the fierce beast when it came in pursuit. The princess is mine!'' ''No, no, no!'' shouted the tailor, jumping up and down. ''Had I not stitched the boat back together, all of us would be lying at the bottom of the sea right now, food for fishes. The princess must wed *me*!''

The king thought for a while and scratched his head. ''You all have strong claims,'' he said, ''and I cannot honestly say that any one of you has more right to the princess than any other. Therefore I will given her to none. But in her place I will bestow on each one of you a half of a kingdom.'' The king was good as his word, and they all lived happily for the rest of their lives.

The Fox and the Horse

A FARMER OWNED a horse. For many years the animal had given good and faithful service, but now it had grown old, and was no longer able to work as it once had. One cold and stormy night, the farmer came to the horse and said to it, "My friend, you have come to the end of your road. Since you can no longer earn your keep, I must turn you out. But you have one chance. If you can bring a lion to me, I will take care of you for the rest of your life."

The sad old beast went out into the rain, without a hope in the world. As he slowly and aimlessly made his way along the road, a fox came up to him. "How now, brother, why so sad?" he asked. The horse told him of his plight. "Cheer up!" said the fox. "If you do as I tell you, everything will turn out well. Just lie down in the road and pretend you are dead." The horse decided he had nothing to lose, and lay down in the middle of the road as though he were dead.

The fox quickly scampered to the home of the lion. "Friend lion," said the fox, "down on the road is a dead horse. If you get to it now, you can make a wonderful meal of it." The lion licked his lips at the thought, and went along with the fox. The two reached the horse, and when the lion was just about to take a bite out of it, the fox pretended that he had an idea. "Friend lion," said the fox, "why should you stand out here and eat in the rain when you could take the horse home with you and dine in comfort? Let me tie his tail to your paws, so you can drag him back home with you."

The lion consented, and the fox tied his paws in the horse's tail. Then he shouted, "Pull, horse, pull!" The horse got up, the lion held prisoner in his tail, and dragged the raging beast back to the farmer's door. When the farmer saw that the horse had brought him a lion he was very pleased. "I made a promise to you," he said to the horse, "and I shall keep it. Come inside, next to the fire. You need work no more, and I shall always provide for your needs." The horse came in and the two lived happily for the rest of their days.

King Thrushbeard

IN A DISTANT KINGDOM, years ago, there lived a king with an arrogant and haughty daughter. When it came time for the princess to marry, the king held a banquet to which he invited many eligible young princes. The princess scorned them all, especially one she named King Thrushbeard, for his pointed beard reminded her of the beak of a thrush.

Soon after, the king lost his patience with his daughter. A beggar was passing the castle and, in a fit of temper, the king gave the princess to him as his wife. The princess screamed and cried, but to no avail. The beggar grasped her firmly by the hand and took her home with him. On the way, they passed a fine city. "Whose city is this?" asked the princess. "It is King Thrushbeard's, and might have been yours," said the beggar, and the princess dropped a tear. Later they passed a fine forest. "Whose forest is this?" asked the princess. "It is King Thrushbeard's, and might have been yours," replied the beggar, and the princess dropped a tear. Finally they came to a dreadful little hovel. "Whose wretched hovel is this?" asked the princess. "It is mine, and you will live in it with me," said the beggar, pushing her inside.

Life was hard for the princess. Not only did she have to do all the household tasks, but because of their great poverty, she also had to try to make some extra money. Her fingers were too delicate to weave baskets. She had not the skill to make pottery. So the beggar got her a position as kitchen

maid at the castle, where she had to do all the dirty work. Occasionally scraps from the table were tossed her way. These she would store in little iron pots which she hid in her dress and took home to feed herself and her beggar husband. This was the only way the two of them were able to survive.

One day, as she was about to return to her hovel at the end of the day's work, she heard the sound of music and laughter coming from the great hall of the castle. Quietly she crept upstairs to see what was happening. A great feast was being given to celebrate the marriage of the eldest princess. The hall was bright, and filled with nobles in rich silks, gleaming gold and flashing jewels. Hiding behind a curtain, the princess watched and wept, thinking of how her proud nature had brought her to such a sad state.

Suddenly a prince, who seemed to the princess the most handsome man she had ever seen, noticed her hiding behind the curtain. He went to her, and told her that he wanted to dance with her. Great was the princess's embarrassment when she saw that he was none other than King Thrushbeard! But he did not seem to recognize her. As she danced with him, the iron pots fell from her ragged dress and clanged against the floor, spilling food all over. Everyone laughed at her. The princess wept with humiliation, and tried to run away. But the guards caught her as she ran down the stairs, and brought her back to King Thrushbeard.

"Do not be afraid," he told her, "for I and the beggar whom you married are the same person. Out of love for you I put on the disguise to teach you humility. You have learned your lesson." The weeping princess sobbed, "I am unworthy to be your wife." But King Thrushbeard kissed her, dried her tears, and the two lived in great happiness.

Sleeping Beauty

THERE ONCE LIVED a queen who
went for many years without child,
to the disappointment of herself and
her husband. One day, as she was
bathing in a pool in the garden, a
frog leaped out of the water and told
her that she would soon have a
daughter.

And so it happened that the queen did give birth, and the whole
kingdom rejoiced. The king gave a lavish christening party to which all the
nobles were invited. He also invited the fairies who lived in his kingdom, for
he wanted them to feel kindly toward the child. But there were thirteen
fairies and the king only had enough golden plates to serve twelve. So one of
them was not invited.

The party was brilliant. Each fairy, making use of her magic power,
bestowed a special gift on the little princess. One bestowed beauty, another a
kind nature, another intelligence. Suddenly, with a crash of thunder and the
smell of smoke, the thirteenth fairy—the fairy who had *not* been invited—appeared in the midst of the revelers. ''How dare you not invite
me?'' she hissed at the cowering king and queen. ''For this you shall pay
dearly. When the princess is fifteen, she will prick her finger on a spindle

and fall dead!'' Howling with laughter, she disappeared as abruptly as she had come.

The court was thunderstruck. But the twelfth fairy, who had not yet bestowed her gift upon the baby, turned to the king. ''I cannot undo the curse,'' she said, ''but I *can* alter it. When the princess is fifteen, she will prick her finger on a spindle, but she will *not* die. She will fally asleep, and slumber for one hundred years, as shall every man and beast in the castle.'' But the king was deathly afraid for his child, and ordered that all the spindles in the kingdom be collected and burned.

The child grew into a beautiful young girl, dearly loved by everyone in the kingdom. But it happened that early on the day of her fifteenth birthday the king and queen had gone out of the castle, leaving the princess alone for a while. In their absence she wandered up and down the hallways of a long-unused part of the castle, trying to find something that would amuse her. She came upon a narrow circular stairway that led to the top of an ancient tower. At the top of the stairs was a door with an aged, rusted key in the lock. As soon as the princess put her hand to the key, the door flew open. Beyond was a dusty little room, in the middle of which sat an old woman doing her spinning.

''Good day,'' said the princess. ''Pray, what are you doing?'' The old lady stopped spinning and said, ''I am spinning, my pet. Would you like to try it?'' The princess was fascinated, for she had never seen a spindle before, and sat down to try her hand at it. As soon as she touched the spindle, she pricked her finger and fell into a magic sleep, as did every man and beast in the castle. The doves fell asleep where they were on the roof, the cook fell asleep as he was about to strike a page for stealing a cake. Horses,

46

dogs, guardsmen, ladies-in-waiting, the king and the queen—all slumbered. Even the fire in the grate flickered and began to snore.

As soon as the castle began its sleep, a hedge of briar roses began to grow up around it. Year by year it grew, ever taller, ever thicker, until eventually it completely hid the castle and its sleeping occupants from view. Bit by bit people began to forget that it had ever existed. There were those,

however, who kept the legend alive. Some foolish princes went into the hedge to try to make their way to the castle, but all of them were stuck fast on the sharp thorns and perished in agony.

Slowly, the hundred years passed. When they were almost up, a young prince chanced to pass through the kingdom. From an old man he heard of the legend of the hidden castle and the princess who lay asleep within it. Even though the old man told him of the many valiant heroes who had lost their lives in the briar hedge, the young prince resolved to make the princess his own. Following the old man's directions, he made his way to the hidden castle.

The briar roses were in full bloom as he approached the hedge. At the very moment he made his way into it, the hundred-year spell was up, and the hedge parted before him that he might pass through without a scratch, closing again behind him.

As he entered the castle he was amazed to see the people and animals, all motionless as though they were statues. After a while he passed into the tower where the princess slept. He cautiously made his way up the stairs and entered the little room. There lay the princess, even more beautiful than he had dared to hope. She was so lovely that he bent over and gave her a kiss. Her eyes fluttered open, and at once she fell in love with him. With that the entire castle came back to life—dogs barked, flies buzzed, the cook finally struck the page and the fire flared up.

The prince led the princess down to her parents, who had awakened in the throne room, and asked for her hand in marriage. This they gave willingly and the two lived happily together for the rest of their lives.

Rapunzel

THERE ONCE LIVED a poor man and his wife, who was about to have a child. One day, the wife looked across a stone wall into a nearby garden. There she saw wonderful vegetables and was driven mad by the wish to eat some of them. So she begged her husband to steal some.

He had climbed over the wall and picked a few vegetables when suddenly Mother Gothel, the powerful witch who owned the garden, appeared. "For your theft, you will pay with your life!" she cried. The poor man begged her to spare him. "Well now," she said. "I know your wife is with child. If you promise to give me the baby when it is born, I shall spare your

life.'' With heavy heart, the poor man agreed. And so, when his wife gave birth to the child, which they named Rapunzel, Mother Gothel snatched the infant away.

When Rapunzel was twelve, and had grown to be most beautiful, the witch took her deep into the forest and locked her in a tiny room at the top of a tower that had neither stairs nor doors and only one small window. Every day Mother Gothel visited Rapunzel. Standing below the window, she would call, ''Rapunzel, Rapunzel, let down your hair.'' The child would wrap her long golden tresses over a hook near the window and, hand over hand, Mother Gothel would climb up.

One day a Prince was passing through the forest, and heard Rapunzel singing a beautiful, lonely song as she sat in her tower. He stopped and listened. Then he saw Mother Gothel approach the tower and climb into the room. After she had left, he went to the bottom of the tower and called, ''Rapunzel, Rapunzel, let down your hair.'' The hair came tumbling down and the Prince climbed. At first Rapunzel was shocked, for she had never seen a man before, but the two soon fell deeply in love. Day after day he visited her, and they planned her escape.

But Mother Gothel discovered their plot. Enraged, she cut off Rapunzel's long hair and sent her far away. The next day, when the Prince called out to Rapunzel, Mother Gothel let down the hair she had cut. When the Prince climbed to the window, the witch pushed him, so that he fell among the thorns, which put out his eyes.

The blind Prince wandered from land to land until, finally, he heard again Rapunzel singing her sad song. He rushed to her and, in her joy, she wept tears that fell on his eyes. At once they became clear and he could see again. The Prince took Rapunzel to his kingdom, and the two lived long and happily together.

Cat and Mouse in Partnership

A MOUSE AND A CAT once met each other. The cat declared that she found the mouse absolutely charming, and suggested that the two of them live together. The mouse thought the idea fine, and the two set up their own little household.

One day the cat said to the mouse, ''You know, the warm weather will not last forever. When winter comes food will be scarce, and unless we make some provision, we may well starve.'' The mouse agreed, and the two went out and bought a pot of fat. They decided that it would be safest in church, so into the church it was put.

But the cat could not put the pot of fat out of her mind. When the desire for it became more than she could bear, she said to the mouse, ''I have been asked to be godmother to my cousin's son, a pretty little striped kitten who has just been born. I must go to the christening today. May I leave and entrust the housework to you?'' The mouse was delighted to help her friend. The cat went out. She crept into the church, opened the pot of fat and ate some off the top. Then she went outside and lay in the sun for a while, washing her whiskers.

The mouse greeted the cat when she came home. ''And what was the dear little thing named?'' she asked. ''Top-off,'' said the cat. The mouse thought that was a strange name.

Only a day had passed before the cat again began to long for the fat. ''My dear,'' she said to the mouse, ''I must go to another christening—this time for a sweet little tabby.'' The mouse bid her go. Off the cat went, and ate a good deal more. Then she went for a little walk about the town walls. On her return, the mouse asked her how things had gone. ''Splendidly,'' said the cat, ''The child has been named Half-gone.'' ''How strange a name,'' thought the mouse.

But the cat could not rest for the thought of the little fat left in the pot. The next day, she said to the mouse, ''Good things come in threes. I have one more christening to go to, and I really cannot refuse.'' So off she went, straight to the fat, which she polished off in no time at all. At home she told the mouse that the kitten had been named All-gone. ''What a very, very peculiar name,'' said the mouse. The cat was irritated by the remark. ''All you do is sit at home in your little gray coat. You know nothing of the world. Just keep your whiskers clean and mind your manners.''

Winter came and supplies of food ran very low. When they were down to their last cracker, the mouse said to the cat, ''I think the time has come for us to go to the church and get the fat. Won't it taste good?'' ''You might just as well stick your tongue out the window,'' mumbled the cat to herself, but she went along with the mouse to the church where they discovered the empty pot. The mouse was no fool, and quickly realized what had happened. ''A fine friend you turned out to be,'' she snorted. ''You ate it all! Top-off, indeed! And Half-gone—'' ''Hold your mouth,'' hissed the cat, ''or I shall eat you as well.'' But the mouse let the name ''All-gone'' slip from her lips and the cat ate her.

Heigh-ho, that's the way of the world.

Fundevogel

A FORESTER ONCE found a baby that had been stolen from its mother by a bird. He took the little boy home with him and named him Fundevogel. The child grew up with the forester's daughter, Lina, and the two became fast friends. One evening Lina saw the old cook, Sanna, carrying buckets of water back from the well. The cook said, ''Tomorrow, when your father is out, I will boil the water and cook Fundevogel in it.'' The frightened Lina went to warn Fundevogel.

In the morning the two children fled together. Sanna ordered three servants to go after them. When the children saw the servants coming, Lina said, ''You must be a rosebush, and I the rosebud upon it.'' So they turned themselves into the rosebush and the rosebud. When the servants returned they told Sanna that they had found nothing save a rosebush. ''Fools,'' cried Sanna, ''you should have destroyed it!'' And she sent them forth again.

This time Lina said to Fundevogel, ''You must become a church and I the chandelier in it.'' This they did, and again the servants returned empty-handed. ''Fools,'' cried Sanna, ''you should have destroyed it!'' And she went forth with them. Seeing them approach, Lina said to Fundevogel, ''You must become a pond, and I the duck that swims upon it.'' This they did, and when Sanna arrived, she tried to drink up the pond. But the duck took her by the nose and drowned her.

The Valiant Little Tailor

MANY YEARS AGO, a little tailor was sitting in his shop, working as he ate lunch. A swarm of buzzing flies flew into the room and bothered the tailor to distraction. So he struck at them with some cloth, killing seven. This impressed the little man so much that he embroidered the words ''seven at one blow'' on his belt, put some old cheese in his pocket and went forth in the world to seek adventures.

Crossing through the mountains, the little tailor met a giant who thought he would make short work of him. But the little tailor said, ''Take care! Read my belt!'' The giant read and, thinking that ''seven'' meant seven men, became more cautious. ''If you are truly so fierce,'' he said, ''give me some proof of your strength.'' The little tailor reached into his pocket and pulled out the cheese. ''Do you see this rock?'' he asked. ''I will squeeze water out of it!'' And he squeezed the cheese till the moisture dripped from it. The giant let the tailor go his way.

Arriving in a foreign kingdom, the little tailor was brought to the king, who promised him the hand of his daughter if he would rid the realm of two evil giants. The tailor found where they slept and climbed into a tree. He then dropped a pebble on the head of one giant. The giant thought his fellow has done it and began to fight with him. They killed each other and thus the valiant little tailor became a prince.

The Queen Bee

THREE PRINCES ONCE set off in search of adventure. The two elder brothers mocked the youngest, whom they called Blockhead, for his nature was simple. As they traveled, they came across an anthill. The elder brothers wanted to destroy it, but Blockhead made them leave the ants alone. Then they saw some ducks swimming, and wanted to roast them, but Blockhead made them leave them alone. When they spied a beehive, they wanted to light a fire and suffocate the bees so that they could take the honey, but Blockhead made them leave the creatures in peace.

Finally the three came to an enchanted castle. A little man in gray told them that three princesses lay asleep within. If the brothers could do three tasks, they would win the princesses. If not, they would be turned to stone.

The first task was to gather a thousand pearls that lay hidden in the moss of the forest. The first two brothers failed, and were turned to stone. But when Blockhead tried, the ants he had saved scurried about and brought the pearls to him. Then he had to get the key to the princesses' room. It lay at the bottom of a lake, and Blockhead was in despair until the ducks he had saved dived into the water and got the key for him. For his final task, Blockhead had to determine which of the princesses was youngest and sweetest. They all looked the same. The only difference was this: at their last meal, the youngest had eaten honey, while the others had eaten some sugar and some syrup. The queen of the bees Blockhead had saved flew into the room and alighted on the lips of the youngest and sweetest princess, for she could still taste the bit of honey. When the prince awoke her, his brothers revived. Blockhead married the youngest and sweetest. Never again did his elder brothers make sport of him.

The Lady and the Lion

ONCE UPON A TIME there was a father who had three daughters. One day, before he went on a trip, he asked them what presents they wanted him to bring back. The two elder daughters wanted jewelry, which was simple enough for the father to get. But the youngest wanted a singing, soaring lark. Before his return, the father had bought the jewelry, but he had not found a lark. As he was passing through a dark forest, he spied one in a tree, climbed up and caught it. At that very moment a lion, howling with rage, came bounding out. "How dare you take my lark," he roared. "Prepare to die!" The man begged to be spared and the lion let him go, on the condition that his youngest daughter be given to him.

When the man returned home, there was great wailing as he told his story. But the youngest daughter did not fear, and went alone into the forest. There she was met by the lion, who took her to his castle, where other lions dwelt. He was a prince under a spell, and took his human form at night, as did his companions. The lion and the maid fell in love, and lived happily together.

One day the lion told the maid that her eldest sister was about to be married, and gave her permission to visit home if she so wanted. The maid refused, unless the lion would come with her. He told her that he dared not, for were single ray of light to touch him, he would turn into a dove and be

forced to fly about the world for seven years. The maid promised she would protect him from the light.

The lion went to the wedding feast, but, as fate would have it, even though the maid tried to shield him from the light, a beam touched him. He turned into a dove and flew away. For seven years the maid endured great hardship trying to find him. Then she found that, human again, he had married an evil princess, who had taken his memory from him. She went to the princess, who envied the maid's gown, which had been given to her by the sun during her wanderings. The princess asked the maid if she would sell it. The maid said she would give it only if she were allowed to enter the prince's room that night. The bargain was struck, but the princess put a drug in his drink. When the maid entered the prince's room, she was unable to rouse him.

The next day the maid showed the princess three eggs which the moon had given her during her wanderings. She broke them open and out ran three golden chicks. The princess wanted them, and the maid gave them on the condition that she again be allowed into the prince's room. But that night the prince did not drink the drug, so when the maid was let into his chamber, he recognized her and told her how he had been enslaved by the princess.

Now the princess's father was a powerful sorcerer, so the prince and the maid quietly slipped away from the palace. They mounted a griffin which bore them over the Red Sea. When the beast became tired, the maid dropped a nut the night wind had given her. At once a tall nut tree grew from the water, and the griffin was able to rest in its branches for the night. In the morning he returned the prince and the maid home safely, and they lived in peace and contentment for the rest of their lives.